nickelodeon™

Dora Helps Swiper

written by Molly Reisner • illustrated by Susan Hall

Reader's
Digest
Children's Books·

New York, New York • Montréal, Québec • Bath, United Kingdom

Dora and her best friend Boots were playing in her yard when they saw Swiper racing toward them. "Oh, mannn! Oh, mannn! Help! Dora, Boots, I was packing for a sleepover at my Grandma's House when a big wind blew all my favorite things out of my wagon!" said Swiper. "My pajamas, puppy book, and Funny Bunny are gone!"

"We'll help you find all your things...but you have to promise not to swipe anybody else's stuff," Dora said.

"I promise," sighed Swiper. They asked Map where to find Swiper's stuff.

"The pajamas are at Crocodile Lake, the puppy book is at the Tangled Forest, and Swiper's Funny Bunny is at Strawberry Hill," said Map.

At Crocodile Lake, Swiper found his pajama trunk. But it was empty!

"The big wind blew my favorite pair of pajamas around the lake," said Swiper. Luckily, there was a raft tied up nearby.

"*¡Vámonos!* Let's hop inside that raft to get your pajamas back. But be on the lookout for crocodiles," said Dora, putting on a life jacket.

Swiper could see his duck pajamas resting on a tiny island in the middle of Crocodile Lake. The friends reached the island and Swiper grabbed his pajamas, but just then, a group of crocodiles started to swim toward the raft.

"Whoa!" yelled Boots. Dora, Boots, and Swiper each grabbed a paddle.

"*¡Rápido!* We need to super-paddle across the lake!" said Dora. They rowed as quickly as they could back to shore.

When they got out of the raft, the friends saw
the Fiesta Trio. They looked worried. "The big
wind blew away our instruments," said the snail.
"And now we can't play music!" added the
grasshopper.

"They should be around here!" said the frog
as he looked under a leaf. Swiper knew how it
felt to lose a favorite thing.

"Don't worry, guys. I'll keep an eye out for
them," promised Swiper.

The friends made it to the Tangled Forest. The trees had numbers on them, but they were all mixed up! Boots pointed to the treetops. "Look at all the stuff up there!" he said. The big wind had blown lots of things into the leaves.

"Oooh, is my puppy book up there?" wondered Swiper.

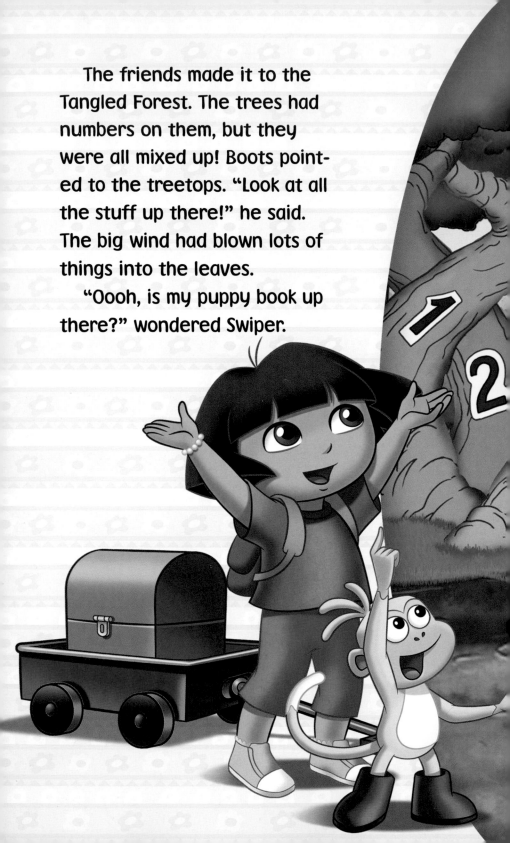

The puppy book was in the trees! Dora looked at the numbers on the tree trunks. "If we put these numbers in order, maybe we can untangle the trees," said Dora. "Let's count!"

"One, two, three, four, five, six," they counted together. Suddenly, the trees untangled and everything that was stuck up there fell down!

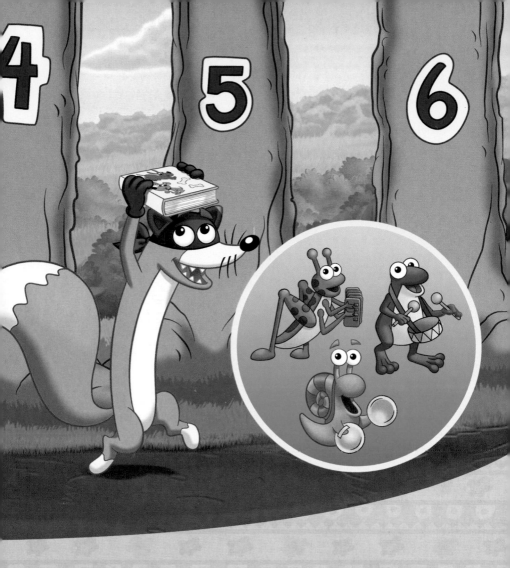

Swiper caught his puppy book. "I got it!" said Swiper. A tiny drum, accordion, and cymbals fell from the trees, too. The Fiesta Trio ran toward their instruments.

"Yippeee!" said the snail.

"Now we can play our music!" said the frog.

"Thanks for helping us find our instruments," said the grasshopper.

Dora, Boots and Swiper raced toward Strawberry Hill.

"I need to find Funny Bunny for my sleepover at Grandma's House!" said Swiper. He looked and looked.

Swiper finally found his Funny Bunny! "I love you!" he said, giving his Funny Bunny a tight squeeze. Suddenly, there was a strong breeze in the air. The friends looked up and saw a windy wind moving toward Grandma's House.

"The big wind is headed right for Grandma's pie on her windowsill!" cried Swiper.

"We need to be really fast to beat the wind," said Dora. Swiper leapt into action!

"Instead of using my arm spins to swipe, I'll use them to keep the wind away!" said Swiper.

He ran up Strawberry Hill, spinning his arms really fast like a windmill. Dora and Boots helped, too. Soon, all the spinning made so much wind that it blew the big wind away! "Yay, we did it!" cheered Boots.

"Good job stopping that windy wind!" said Grandma, giving Swiper a hug. She was very proud of Swiper.

"Do you want to stay for my sleepover?" Swiper asked Dora and Boots. They checked with their parents, and they said yes!

"Thanks for helping me find my favorite things for my sleepover," said Swiper.

"You did a good job not swiping today," said Boots.

They all chose their favorite pajamas to wear and ate some of Grandma's tasty strawberry pie.

This was the best sleepover Swiper ever had!